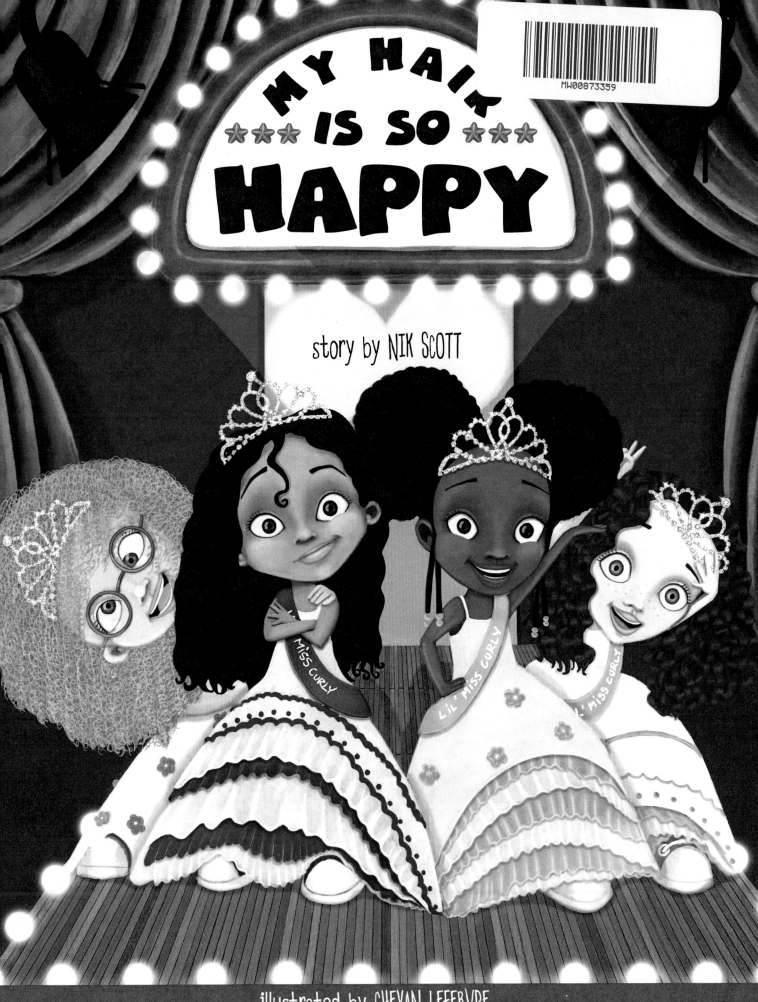

MY HAIR
*** IS SO ***
# HAPPY

story by NIK SCOTT

illustrated by CHEYAN LEFEBVRE

My Hair Is So Happy

Text copyright © 2012 Nik Scott
Illustrations copyright © 2013 Cheyan Lefebvre

Published by JAS Publishing Co.

iNIKSCOTT.com
Life Happens. Don't Conform.

ISBN-13: 978-0615925554
ISBN-10: 0615925553

For Delilah

Twisted, braided

or big and free,

my hair is so happy !

Loc'd, cornrowed

or wet and coily,

my hair is so happy !

Wavy, pressed

or kinky-curly,

my hair is so happy !

In pony tails, in beads

or soft and puffy,

my hair is so happy !

...TO HAPPINESS

An interview with Hope

Colorful barrettes, silky bows--
I call them hair candy !

My hair is so happy !

When I get it done,
it doesn't bother me

My hair is so happy !

Everywhere I go, people say
"It's so pretty !"

My hair is so happy !

On a windy day,

blowing in the breeze,

my hair is so happy !

In the sunshine,

laying on the beach,

my hair is so happy !

Dancing outside

while it's raining,

my hair is so happy !

Hiking, camping,

fishing or when I go skiing,

my hair is so happy !

Painting, reading or watching a movie,
my hair is so happy !

Yes I love my hair, it's amazing !

My hair is so happy !

All of me was made fearfully
and wonderfully !

Don't worry be curly!

My hair is so happy !

And the best thing about my hair...

... It's what
God gave me !

PROMISE

Lil' Miss Curly
Contest

My hair is so happy !

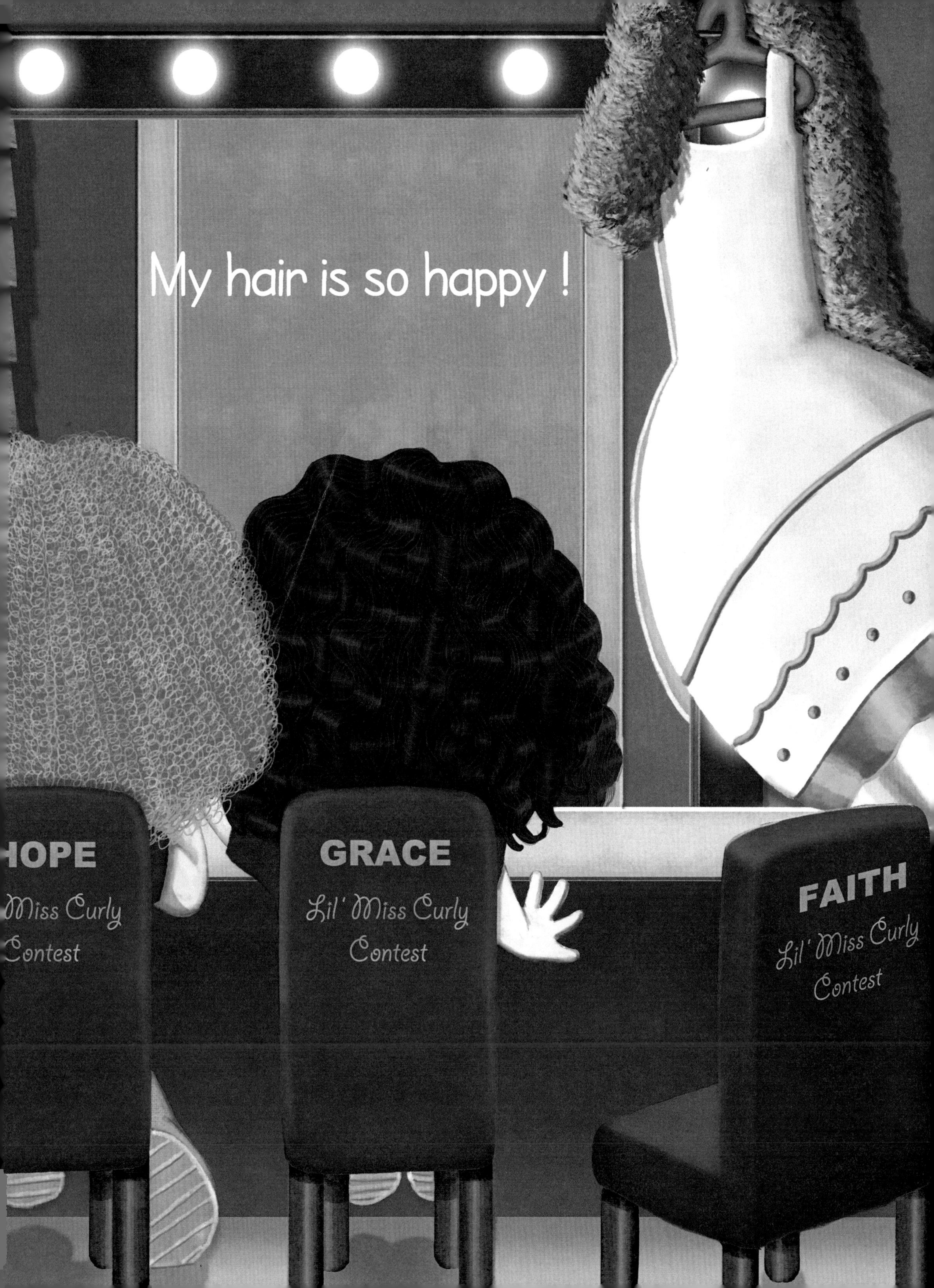

Made in United States
North Haven, CT
14 July 2022

21393021R00022